Make friends with

The little pony with the big heart

Sheltie is the lovable little Shetland pony with a big personality. His best friend and owner is Emma, and together they have lots of exciting adventures.

Share Sheltie and Emma's adventures in

SHELTIE THE SHETLAND PONY
SHELTIE SAVES THE DAY
SHELTIE AND THE RUNAWAY
SHELTIE FINDS A FRIEND
SHELTIE TO THE RESCUE
SHELTIE IN DANGER
SHELTIE RIDES TO WIN
SHELTIE AND THE SADDLE MYSTERY
SHELTIE LEADS THE WAY
SHELTIE THE HERO
SHELTIE IN TROUBLE
SHELTIE AND THE STRAY
SHELTIE AND THE SNOW PONY

Peter Clover was born and went to school in London. He was a storyboard artist and illustrator before he began to put words to his pictures. He enjoys painting, travelling, cooking and keeping fit, and lives on the coast in Somerset.

Also by Peter Clover in Puffin

The Sheltie series

Sheltie
The Big Surprise

Peter Clover

PUFFIN BOOKS

Special thanks to Jacqui Farley

To Fiona, Isabella and Rosamund

PUFFIN BOOKS

Published by the Penguin Group
Penguin Books Ltd, 27 Wrights Lane, London W8 5TZ, England
Penguin Putnam Inc., 375 Hudson Street, New York, New York 10014, USA
Penguin Books Australia Ltd, Ringwood, Victoria, Australia
Penguin Books Canada Ltd, 10 Alcorn Avenue, Toronto, Ontario, Canada M4V 3B2
Penguin Books (NZ) Ltd, Private Bag 102902, NSMC, Auckland, New Zealand

Penguin Books Ltd, Registered Offices: Harmondsworth, Middlesex, England

First published 1999
1 3 5 7 9 10 8 6 4 2

Created by Working Partners Ltd, London, W12 7QY

The moral right of the author has been asserted

Set in 14/22 Palatino

Made and printed in England by Clays Ltd, St Ives plc

British Library Cataloguing in Publication Data
A CIP catalogue record for this book is available from the British Library

ISBN 0-141-30472-3

Contents

Rabbits
Galore

Chapter One

'I think we have a blackbirds' nest in the cherry tree,' said Dad as he sat down at the kitchen table. 'Joshua and I are going to take a closer look later.'

Emma's little brother, Joshua, clapped his hands and giggled with excitement.

'And what are you and Sheltie going to do this morning?' asked Mum.

3

'I think we'll go for a ride through the village,' said Emma. She put her cereal bowl and spoon in the sink and hurried outside.

It was the start of the Easter holidays and Emma had two whole weeks off school. Emma loved the holidays because it meant she could spend more time with Sheltie, her little Shetland pony.

Sheltie was waiting by the paddock fence. When he saw Emma coming towards him with his bridle on her shoulder he became quite frisky and excited. Suddenly Sheltie realized that Emma wasn't going off to school this morning.

'Come on, boy. Let's go for a ride,' said Emma when she had finished putting on his tack. She gave Sheltie's neck a good scratch, then climbed into the saddle.

As they rode up the lane, Emma noticed that some posters had been pasted along the low wall and on the post by the little stone bridge. She pulled back on Sheltie's reins to stop him so she could read what the posters said.

'Look, Sheltie!' said Emma excitedly. 'There's going to be a special celebration in Little Applewood. Waldo the Magnificent, a famous magician, is coming for one special performance of his Spring Magic Spectacular on Easter Saturday.'

Sheltie looked at the poster and cocked his head to one side. Then he gave a loud blow and shook out his mane. Sheltie had seen Emma's neighbour, Mr Crock, coming towards them over the stone bridge.

'Hello, Emma,' said Mr Crock. 'What are you two up to?'

'Hello, Mr Crock. I was just reading this poster about the magic show,' said Emma.

Sheltie gave Mr Crock a friendly nuzzle with his nose.

'Hello, Sheltie,' said Mr Crock, ruffling his forelock. 'It's a lovely day. I thought you'd be off riding on the moors with Sally and Minnow.'

Sally was Emma's best friend. And Minnow, her pony, was Sheltie's best pony friend.

'Sally's gone off to Rilchester to stay with her gran for Easter,' said Emma. 'So we were going to ride through the village today and over to the East Downs.'

'Well, I've just been to the post office,' said Mr Crock with a big grin. 'There was a reporter in there. And he told me that the local paper is taking photos of Waldo the Magnificent in Mr

Brown's field this morning to advertise the magic show. I'm going along there right now to watch. Do you want to join me?'

'Ooh, that sounds fun, doesn't it, Sheltie?' said Emma.

Sheltie tossed his head impatiently. He didn't know what Emma had said, but he knew he had been standing still for too long. He was eager to be off.

'Let's go to Mr Brown's field to see the magician, Sheltie!' said Emma. She pulled on the reins to turn him around.

Sheltie didn't mind where he went, as long as he was going *somewhere*! The little pony trotted along happily beside Mr Crock, towards the field.

Mr Crock unhooked the gate and

held it open for Emma and Sheltie to ride through.

Mr Brown was in the field watching the preparations for the photo shoot.

'Hello, Mr Brown,' called Emma. 'Will it be all right if we watch?'

Sheltie blew a loud raspberry. That was his way of saying hello too!

'Good morning, Emma, Sheltie, Mr Crock,' said the farmer. He gave Sheltie a stroke. 'Of course you can, Emma. Just keep this one under control.'

Sheltie sniffed Mr Brown's pocket.

'Are you after my peppermints?' he laughed, patting his pockets. Mr Brown found a large white mint which he palmed to the little Shetland pony. Sheltie crunched it noisily.

'Is that Waldo the Magnificent?' asked Emma, pointing towards a short man with glasses.

'No, that's the reporter,' said Mr Brown. 'Waldo is the tall man over there with the big moustache.'

Waldo the Magnificent was unloading boxes from his van. They looked like animal boxes, the kind that people use to carry cats and small dogs in. Waldo was a tall, thin man with a huge waxed moustache. He wore a dark suit and had a long cape lined with red satin draped across his shoulders. A pretty young lady stood beside him holding a beautiful diamond bracelet. It sparkled in the sunlight.

'That's Mandy, Waldo's assistant,'

said Mr Brown. 'The diamonds she's holding are on loan from a jewellery shop in Rilchester. They're going to be in the photos because Waldo will make them disappear during the magic show.'

'What a sweet little horse!' squealed

Mandy as she hurried across the grass towards them.

'He's not a horse,' said Emma with a smile. 'Sheltie is a Shetland pony.'

'Whatever he is, he's adorable,' said Mandy. 'Could we use him in the photos, Waldo?'

Sheltie tossed his head and sniffed Mandy's pocket to see if *she* had any peppermints. Then he sneezed. Mandy's pocket smelt of perfume.

Waldo walked across to meet Sheltie.

'He's a very handsome pony, isn't he?' Waldo gave Emma a friendly smile. 'I had one just like him when I was a lad.'

'What happened to him?' asked Emma.

'Oh, I suddenly shot up and grew too tall for him,' smiled the magician.

Emma grinned and looked up at Waldo. He *was* very tall. Emma couldn't imagine him ever riding a little Shetland pony.

'Can we make the pony disappear instead of the rabbit?' said Mandy. Then she explained to Emma and the others: 'We're going to do a trick from the show for the reporter and photographer so that they can write about it in the newspaper.'

'I don't think Sheltie would like that,' said Emma. She didn't think *she* would like Sheltie to disappear either.

'He may be small but he's a bit too big for the disappearing box,' said Waldo. 'But perhaps he could hold the magic wand in his teeth when we make the rabbit disappear.'

'Sheltie would like that,' said Emma. 'Wouldn't you, boy?'

Sheltie blew a rasping snort and jangled his bit.

'Great,' said Mandy. 'I'll have a word with the reporter.'

'We'll have Sheltie performing magic tricks in no time,' laughed Waldo.

But Sheltie was still busy sniffing pockets and looking for peppermints. Suddenly he found an interesting corner of cloth poking out of Waldo's trousers and snatched at it with his teeth. A green handkerchief whooshed out, then came a red one. Sheltie pulled harder. A blue handkerchief followed. And then a yellow one.

Sheltie pulled until ten handkerchiefs had come out, tied together in a long line. Then Sheltie gave a loud whinny and shook his head. The hankies fluttered about like a multicoloured streamer.

'It looks as if Sheltie can already perform magic tricks!' cried Mr Brown.

Everyone laughed.

'Bring Sheltie around to the side of Waldo,' said Mandy. 'Waldo will give the pony the magic wand to hold in his teeth.'

Emma beamed with delight at Mandy. She was so pleased that they were both going to be in the photographs.

'We're going to be in the newspaper, Sheltie!' Emma whispered.

Emma felt a little shy in front of everyone. She blushed and shuffled her feet. But Sheltie didn't look shy at all. He held his head high and whickered. He was really enjoying all this attention.

The trick went very well. Each time Waldo finished using the magic wand, he gave it to Sheltie to hold in his teeth. Then he pretended he had forgotten where it was.

The reporter was busy jotting things down in his notebook. And his photographer was dashing all around Waldo, adjusting her camera and taking pictures.

Mandy held up a white rabbit.

'This is Snowy,' she said.

She fastened the diamond bracelet around Snowy's neck. It fitted perfectly. Then Waldo put Snowy inside the magic box and waved his magic wand. When the box was opened, Snowy had vanished.

Then suddenly, there was a small

puff of smoke and twenty-one white
rabbits appeared in the field. They all
hopped towards Waldo. Snowy was
with them, the diamond bracelet
glinting in the sun.

'How on earth did he do that?' Mr
Crock cried in astonishment.

'Magic!' said Emma.

Chapter Two

Everyone clapped their hands and Waldo stepped back to take a bow. As he swept up his cloak in a big flourish, he knocked over the table. The disappearing box crashed on to the grass with a loud bang.

'Oh no!' cried Waldo.

The rabbits all scattered in panic as everyone rushed forward to help pick up the disappearing box.

Sheltie danced back out of the way
with a loud snort. Emma held his reins
firmly and kept him very still.

Suddenly Emma realized that all the
rabbits had vanished. Not one was left
in the field.

'The rabbits have all run away!'
cried Emma.

'Oh no,' said Mr Brown. 'I've got

enough trouble with wild rabbits eating my spring crops. Now there are twenty-two tame ones loose in my field as well!'

'I'd better get back to my vegetable garden,' said Mr Crock with a worried frown. 'I hope I get there before the rabbits do!'

'What about the diamonds?' cried Waldo. 'We've got to find Snowy!'

When Emma and Sheltie returned after lunch, they helped to search the field all afternoon. But not a single rabbit could be found.

'I really must find Snowy,' said Waldo. 'The diamond bracelet was only borrowed. It's worth a fortune and I have to return it to the jeweller.'

'All the rabbits must be found too,' said Mr Brown firmly. 'I don't want them loose in my field. You promised me this wouldn't happen.'

'They were probably scared by the loud crash when the table fell over,' said Emma. 'Perhaps they'll turn up when everything quietens down.'

'I hope so,' said Mr Brown. 'I don't want to lose my spring crops to hungry rabbits.'

'I'll ride Sheltie up the lane and see if any of them are hiding in the hedgerows,' said Emma.

She climbed into the saddle and rode slowly towards home.

Halfway along, Sheltie stopped and pricked up his ears. He sniffed the hedgerow and made a snuffling whicker. Sheltie had found something!

But when Emma slipped out of the saddle and searched, she couldn't find any rabbits. Just a family of tiny field mice huddled in a nest.

'We're searching for rabbits, Sheltie,' she said. 'Not mice.'

Sheltie gave a loud blow and sniffed the hedgerow again. He pawed the ground with his hoof. When she looked closely for a second time, Emma saw some white fur caught on a twig.

'Some of the rabbits must have come this way after all,' she said. 'You are clever, Sheltie!'

Emma climbed back into Sheltie's saddle and rode on, watching carefully for any signs of the rabbits. When they reached Sheltie's paddock, they turned around, ready to go back to Mr Brown's field.

But suddenly Sheltie neighed and dashed towards the paddock gate. He propped his chin on the top bar of the wooden fence and stared into his field. Sheltie's paddock was full of white rabbits! They were everywhere.

'We've found them!' whispered Emma. She slid quietly out of the saddle and led Sheltie through the paddock gate. She tried to catch some of the rabbits but they were much too fast for her.

Sheltie ran here, there and everywhere, trying to round up the rabbits and herd them towards Emma.

But each time he got them grouped together, they would hop off frantically in different directions. Sheltie did look funny and Emma couldn't stop laughing.

Then Mum appeared at the kitchen door to see what all the fuss was about. The rabbits scattered again,

disappearing one by one into the hedgerow along the far side of the paddock fence.

'What on earth are you doing?' said Mum.

'Rounding up white rabbits,' laughed Emma.

'I can't see any rabbits,' said Mum.

'Oh no! They've all gone again,' groaned Emma. 'We'll never catch them now!'

Mum looked puzzled and went back into the kitchen, closing the door behind her. Emma hurried over to the hedgerow to search for the rabbits, but they really had disappeared.

Emma rode Sheltie back to the field to tell Mr Brown what they had seen. The farmer and Waldo were still searching for rabbits along the edge of the field. So far they had found nothing.

'I can't understand how they can all disappear like that,' said Mr Brown.

'Just like magic,' said Waldo, scratching his head.

'We must find them,' Mr Brown insisted.

'Perhaps we can get people from the village to help. We could have an Easter rabbit hunt,' suggested Emma.

'Now, that's a brilliant idea, Emma,' said Waldo. 'Do you think many people would come along?'

'If you gave an Easter egg as a prize for each rabbit found,' said Emma, 'then I'm sure all the children would come along!'

'How can we tell everyone about it?' asked Waldo.

'That's easy,' said Mr Brown. 'Just put up a notice next to the village green.'

'And in the post-office window,' said Emma. 'By tomorrow morning, the whole village will know about it!'

It was teatime when Emma turned Sheltie out into his paddock. She padlocked the gate and went into the cottage.

It was grilled sausages and mash for tea, and as she tucked in, Emma continued her lunchtime story for her little brother, Joshua, telling him more about the rabbits and the photographs for the local paper.

'Wabbits!' laughed Joshua.

'You'll be famous now,' said Mum.

'Sheltie and Emma are already famous in Little Applewood.' Dad smiled. 'Everyone knows them.'

'But with all those rabbits loose somewhere near his field,' Emma went on, 'Mr Brown is worried that they'll eat his spring crops. So there's going to be an Easter rabbit hunt tomorrow, with Easter-egg prizes for anyone who catches a rabbit.'

'Ooh! That sounds like fun,' said Mum. 'We can take Joshua along to help.'

Chapter Three

Next morning Emma was up bright and early. She threw back the curtains and looked out at Sheltie, as she did every morning.

But Sheltie wasn't in his usual place by the paddock fence looking up at her. Instead he was gazing at the hedgerow that grew along the far end of the paddock, with his head tilted on one side.

Emma craned her neck to see what he could be looking at, but she couldn't see anything.

'Breakfast's ready, Emma,' called Mum.

'Coming,' Emma said, hurrying downstairs.

After breakfast, Emma went into the paddock to feed Sheltie and get him ready for the rabbit hunt. She put on his tack and was just leading him out of the paddock as Mum, Dad and Joshua joined her.

'It's a shame Sally's gone to stay with her gran,' said Dad. 'She'd really enjoy this.'

'We'll try to win an extra Easter egg for Sally though, won't we, Sheltie?' said Emma. She ruffled Sheltie's mane and he swished his tail.

There was quite a crowd of villagers in Mr Brown's field when they arrived. The reporter and photographer from the local paper had come back to report on the rabbit hunt. This story was turning out better than they had thought.

Everyone gathered at the far end of the field. Waldo the Magnificent stood on a chair to speak.

'Thank you all for coming here this morning,' he began. 'Anyone returning the diamond bracelet worn by Snowy the rabbit will receive one hundred pounds as a reward!' The magician pointed to a large rabbit pen that had been put up in the field. 'Please put the rabbits in the pen when you find them and collect a ticket for each one you bring.' The tickets were in a bucket beside the pen.

'Did you hear that, Sheltie?' said Emma. 'One hundred pounds! I could buy you a new head collar with your name on and still have enough left for tickets to see the magic show on Saturday.'

Sheltie shuffled on the spot and whinnied. He was eager to get started!

Waldo waved a green flag as a signal for the hunt to begin and everyone ran off to search the field for rabbits. Some people had brought pots and pans to bang, hoping that the noise would flush the rabbits out into the open. They went round to the other side of the hedgerow and made quite a racket.

'That noise is more likely to frighten
the rabbits away,' said Mr Brown,
shaking his head.

Sheltie had a wonderful time
galloping around the field trying to
round up the children as they went
chasing down the field.

'Stop it, Sheltie,' giggled Emma. 'It's rabbits we want to catch!'

But not a single rabbit appeared in the field all morning. Some of the villagers got fed up and went home. Others started to picnic on the grass.

'Come and have some lunch, Emma,' called Dad.

Emma's mum and dad had brought a picnic basket with lots of sandwiches, bags of crisps, apples and a cold drink for each of them.

'There are some chunks of apple for you, Sheltie,' said Emma. She held them in her palm for Sheltie to nibble. Then Emma tucked Sheltie's reins into his bridle and let him roam around the field grazing. He was perfectly safe in

Mr Brown's field. He wandered about, nosing into everyone's picnic.

'Sheltie!'

'Over here, Sheltie!' Some of the children called out to him. Sheltie was really enjoying all the attention.

Suddenly, he pricked up his ears. He seemed to be listening to something. He sniffed the air and quickly trotted back to Emma.

'I haven't got anything else for you,' she said when Sheltie nudged her shoulder. 'You'll get tummy-ache if you eat any more!'

Emma was just about to crunch a crisp when a white rabbit hopped out of the hedge right in front of her! Sheltie dashed after it. Another rabbit appeared, then another. Both went running across the field from one side to the other.

Suddenly white rabbits were popping up all over the field.

Emma jumped up and ran after Sheltie.

'Wait for me, Sheltie!' she called.

Sheltie was dashing about, not knowing which way to go first. There were so many rabbits to chase! He herded one successfully towards Emma and watched as she scooped it up into her arms.

'I've got it!' she cried.

Sheltie blew a loud snort.

'Well done!' said Waldo.

Sheltie followed Emma to the pen and watched her pop the rabbit inside. Other people started leaping to their feet, picnics forgotten, in the rush to catch the magician's rabbits.

Sheltie dashed all over the field, rounding rabbits up into little groups and herding them towards the pen, where Emma just picked them up and popped them in.

'Look at all the rabbits following Sheltie,' laughed one of the boys.

'Don't look at them, grab them!' grinned Emma.

Every time Sheltie turned round, he saw rabbits following him, hopping behind him in a game of follow the leader. But when he turned about to face them, they would all hop off in different directions!

'That was amazing!' said Emma, when at last all the rabbits were

caught. 'I think we have the most tickets, Sheltie!'

'Emma and Sheltie have caught ten rabbits!' announced Waldo. 'How will you manage to eat all those Easter eggs?'

'Well,' said Emma, 'I'll keep one for me, one for my friend Sally, and one for my baby brother, Joshua. And the rest I'll share with my other friends.'

Sheltie nudged Emma as if to say,
'What about me?'

'You're not supposed to eat
chocolate, Sheltie!' Emma laughed.
'But you can have a little piece of
mine.'

Altogether twenty-one rabbits had
been found and safely placed in the
pen. But there was still no sign of
Snowy. Or the valuable diamond
bracelet.

Chapter Four

Everyone searched for Snowy until teatime, eager to win the hundred-pound reward. But the rabbit with the diamonds was nowhere to be found, so people packed up and went home.

Emma rode Sheltie back to his paddock and began removing his tack. She had just finished taking off his saddle when he started to fidget.

Sheltie stamped his hoofs and did a funny little dance.

'Keep still, Sheltie,' said Emma. 'I'll soon have your saddle off and you can have a good roll in the grass.'

Sheltie gave a loud blow and pulled on his reins, nodding his head at the hedgerow. Sheltie's ears were pricked and alert.

'Did you hear something, boy?' said Emma.

She knelt down by the hedge and parted it carefully. Something white was hiding deep inside.

'It's Snowy!' gasped Emma. She reached her arm inside. Snowy, with the diamonds flashing around her neck, dashed out into the paddock followed by a very large brown buck rabbit. 'Oh, look, Sheltie! She's found a friend.'

Sheltie's bright eyes sparkled as they watched the two rabbits playing in the field.

Snowy and the big rabbit hopped around for a few moments and then slipped back into the hedgerow further along. Emma bent down to see where they had gone. To her surprise she found even more rabbits. A wild doe and two tiny babies. The doe looked very unhappy and hopped around in worried circles.

Sheltie nudged Emma's hand with his nose. He had seen something else. When she looked towards him, Emma saw some wire netting, like the kind Mr Brown used for repairing the fencing. Sheltie scraped the ground with his hoof. There was another baby rabbit caught in the netting!

'Oh no, you poor thing,' said Emma. She unwrapped the netting very carefully. The baby rabbit wriggled and struggled, but finally Emma got it loose. She screwed the piece of netting up into a tight ball in the palm of her hand and stuffed it in her pocket, out of harm's way.

The baby rabbit hopped towards its mother. Then the rabbits all dashed along the side of the hedge and vanished. All except Snowy, who looked up at Sheltie and twitched her nose.

'Snowy!' Emma called softly.

The rabbit hopped over to her and

Emma was able to scoop her up in her arms. The big brown buck appeared from under the hedgerow and looked at Snowy with bright eyes. Snowy wriggled in Emma's lap and tried to get away.

'I think Snowy wants to stay here with her new friends, Sheltie,' said Emma.

Sheltie whickered and nudged Emma's shoulder.

'I suppose we could return the bracelet *without* Snowy,' said Emma.

Emma carefully removed the diamond bracelet from Snowy's neck and opened her hands to let the rabbit go. Snowy darted off quickly, straight towards the buck, and vanished into the hedgerow.

'Let's go and find Waldo,' said Emma.

Sheltie tossed his head and gave a loud snort when Emma put his saddle back on and tightened the girth strap. He loved to go out for rides. Then she mounted up and rode down the lane to Mr Brown's field.

Waldo was looking very sad when Emma reached him. He was just climbing into his car as Emma and Sheltie trotted up. Emma gave the magician a beaming grin and held out her hand.

'You've found the diamond bracelet!' cried Waldo. 'That's fantastic. Thank you so much.'

'It was Sheltie who found it really,' said Emma. 'He was the one who first noticed something in the hedgerow.'

'But what about Snowy?' asked Waldo. 'What's happened to *her*?'

'I'm sorry,' said Emma. 'But she darted away when I took off the necklace.' It wasn't really a fib. Snowy

had run off when Emma had put her
down.

'Oh dear,' said Waldo sadly. 'I hope
she's going to be all right.'

'I'm sure she will be,' said Emma.

'Well, here is your reward,' said
Waldo, handing her an envelope. 'I
can't thank you and Sheltie enough for
your help.'

*

Next day Mum took Emma into Little
Applewood. They were going to order
a new head-collar for Sheltie with
some of Emma's reward money. And
Emma was going to treat her whole
family to tickets to the Spring Magic
Spectacular. And because the weather
was fine, the show was going to be
held outside on the village green. So
Sheltie was going along too.

At the show there was an extra
special surprise for Sheltie and Emma.
Waldo the Magnificent asked them to
come on to the stage and help out with
a trick.

Sheltie held the magic wand in his
teeth and Emma pulled some sausages
out of Waldo's pocket instead of the

hankies that were supposed to be there. Then Waldo produced the string of hankies from behind Sheltie's ear!

Sheltie was a huge success and made everyone laugh when he shook his head while holding the magic wand. It looked as if he were waving it like a magician!

As for Snowy, there were lots of sightings of a white rabbit in the fields of Little Applewood, but no one ever

caught her. After all, she was a
magician's rabbit, and very good at
vanishing!

Sheltie's
Sheep

Chapter One

'Look, Emma!' said Dad. 'I think
the blackbird eggs have hatched.'
He pointed to the cherry tree at the
back of their cottage, by Sheltie's
paddock.

Emma looked at the nest, which
was hidden among the leaves on a
branch high up in the tree. She could
see the mother bird going busily to
and from the nest.

'She must be bringing food to her babies,' said Emma.

'Hungry,' said Joshua, Emma's little brother.

Sheltie rested his head on the top bar of the paddock fence and gave a soft blow. Then he stretched his neck as if trying to see the baby birds.

'I wonder how many eggs have hatched,' said Emma as the mother bird flew off again.

Suddenly, something woolly came tearing down the lane and dashed towards the cottage. It ran like a streak of white lightning.

'What on earth . . .' said Dad.

It veered away from the cottage and headed round the back towards the paddock, where Dad, Emma and Joshua were standing.

As it got nearer they could see that it was a fluffy white sheep!

'Come back,' cried a voice. 'Stop!'

A boy came running towards them. He leaped forward and made a grab for the sheep, but it dodged through the gate and into Sheltie's paddock.

Then it dashed across the grass towards Sheltie, who was now grazing near his field shelter. The sheep had its head down and wasn't looking where it was going.

Sheltie suddenly looked up as Emma called: 'Look out, Sheltie!'

The little pony pranced out of the way just in the nick of time. He gave a surprised whinny and tossed his head.

The sheep slowed down and stopped when it came to the field shelter and peeped inside cautiously. When it saw the shelter was empty, it quickly disappeared inside.

Sheltie stared after it with his head cocked to one side. Then he galloped over to his shelter to see what was going on. The sheep took no notice of

him. It was helping itself to hay from the hay net.

The boy stopped when he reached the paddock gate, gasping for breath. He was just a bit taller than Emma, with curly blond hair and blue eyes.

'Can I have my sheep back, please?' he asked politely.

'Of course you can,' said Dad. 'That sheep gave you quite a chase, didn't it?'

'We call her Lightning Nellie. She's always running off,' said the boy.

Sheltie poked his head inside the field shelter and gave Nellie a friendly whicker. He was very curious about this sheep. Nellie continued to eat Sheltie's hay.

'My name's Emma,' said Emma. 'What's your name?'

'I'm Joe Tomlinson,' said the boy. 'I live at Burdock Farm on the other side of the moor.'

'What's Lightning Nellie doing in Little Applewood?' asked Emma.

'Our sheep usually graze on the moor, but Nellie has taken a sudden liking to Little Applewood,' explained Joe. 'This is the third time that she's found her way down here. Mr Crock is a friend of my dad. He saw Nellie outside his gate and phoned us. My dad is waiting down the lane for me.'

'I bet Mr Crock was worried about his vegetables,' said Emma. 'He's very proud of them and would be upset if they ended up as a sheep's breakfast!'

'Nellie prefers Mr Crock's lawn!' Joe grinned. 'Nellie's going to have a lamb soon. My dad thinks that she's looking for a quiet place to have her baby. She'd be much safer on the moor where we can check on her. But Dad thinks she has Little Applewood in mind.'

'Well, we'd better fetch Nellie before

she causes any more trouble,' said
Emma.

She led Joe inside the paddock and
Sheltie galloped over. He butted
Emma gently with his head, nudging
her towards his field shelter. He
wanted to show her his new friend,
Nellie the sheep.

'This is Sheltie,' smiled Emma.

'He's a beauty,' said Joe admiringly.
He reached out a hand and let Sheltie
sniff his palm. Then he rubbed
Sheltie's ears.

Sheltie seemed to like Joe. He
nudged Joe with his nose.

Emma and Joe walked over to the
field shelter where Nellie was just
finishing her snack. Joe gently held on
to her soft coat and slipped a collar

over her head. Then he tied a long piece of rope to the collar and led Nellie out of the field shelter. She seemed quite well behaved as she trotted along behind him.

Sheltie danced forward when Nellie passed by and gave a loud snort. The funny sheep answered with a bleat.

'I hope Nellie stays where she's supposed to this time,' said Emma.

'I hope so too,' said Joe. 'See you!'

Joe closed the paddock gate behind him and led Nellie off down the lane.

Chapter Two

The next morning Emma had work to do. She pulled on her boots and went outside to clean out Sheltie's field shelter. It was her job to make sure he had a nice clean place to live. It took her half the morning to muck out the shelter and replace the straw bedding. Sheltie liked to play when Emma was in his shelter and he made the cleaning take twice as long as it should have

done. He grabbed the broom with his
teeth and tried to play tug with it.
Then he knocked over the bucket of
water. But Emma didn't mind.

'Emma!' Mum called from the
cottage. 'Sally is on the phone for you.'

Emma hurried inside and came back
to the paddock five minutes later with

Sheltie's tack over her arm. As soon as Sheltie saw his saddle he began to dance around excitedly.

Emma looked up at the cloudy sky.

'I hope it doesn't rain,' she said. 'Sally just phoned to say that she's back from Rilchester and is on her way over. We're going to go for a picnic, Sheltie.'

Sally was Emma's best friend. She and her pony, Minnow, lived at Fox Hall Manor, on the other side of the orchard.

Sheltie gave a loud blow. He was eager to get going.

Emma slipped on his bridle and Sheltie opened his mouth to take the bit. She placed the saddle on Sheltie's back and was just about to tighten the

girth around his fat tummy when she
heard hoofs clattering along in the
distance.

Sheltie got very excited when he
heard the hoofs and saw Minnow
trotting along the lane. He became
quite frisky and wouldn't stand
still for Emma to tighten his girth
strap.

'If you don't keep still, Sheltie, we'll
never be ready to go,' said Emma.

Sheltie blew a raspberry and stood
very still while Emma finally
tightened the strap and stood up to
greet Sally and Minnow.

'Hello, Sally,' called Emma.

Sheltie tossed his head excitedly.

'Hello,' said Sally. 'We've brought
Sheltie a present. I got it in Rilchester

last week, when I was staying with my gran.' She held out something wrapped in a yellow cloth for Sheltie to see.

Sheltie seemed to think that the cloth was his present and grabbed a corner with his teeth. He snatched it away and galloped off in a mad dash around the paddock with the yellow cloth flapping like a flag. The present that had been wrapped in the cloth tumbled out on to the ground.

Sheltie raced here, there and everywhere. The cloth dangled from his mouth and his eyes shone, full of mischief, beneath his bushy fringe. The girls laughed. Sheltie looked so funny waving his 'flag'.

When he galloped back, Emma

grabbed the cloth and pulled hard. Sheltie pulled back.

'I'm not playing tug of war, Sheltie,' said Emma. 'Give the cloth back to Sally.'

'That isn't your present, Sheltie,' laughed Sally. Emma handed her the 'thing' that had fallen on to the grass. 'We brought you a salt lick to keep in your shelter.'

Sally held out a square block of salt.
Sheltie sniffed it and then rasped his
tongue along it, making Sally's fingers
all wet. She giggled and handed the
salt lick back to Emma.

Emma carried it to the field shelter
and slid it into a special metal holder
that was already screwed to the wall.
Sheltie pranced along behind her,

trying to give the block little licks. He loved the salty taste.

'Thanks, Sally,' said Emma. 'And you too, Minnow.'

Emma untucked Sheltie's reins from his bridle and led him out of the paddock.

Sheltie stretched his neck up and gave Minnow a friendly nuzzle with his nose. He was always pleased to see his best friend.

Minnow rested his chin on the top of Sheltie's head and gave a soft blow of greeting.

Emma hoisted herself up on to Sheltie's back.

'Which way shall we go?' asked Emma.

'Let's take the bridle path that leads straight up to the moor,' said Sally. 'My dad said there are lots of sheep up there and lots of newborn lambs.'

'That's a great idea,' beamed Emma. 'We might see Joe and Nellie the sheep. We met them yesterday.'

After Emma had told Sally all about Nellie, Sheltie led the way along the lane to the bridle path that would lead them right up to the moor.

*

It was nearly lunchtime when the two ponies arrived on the edge of the moor.

Emma and Sally slipped from their saddles and hooked their ponies' reins loosely over a bush, letting Sheltie and Minnow graze on the long grass.

Sheltie snatched up a mouthful of red clover and munched it hungrily.

Emma sat on the grass and Sally unpacked the picnic food.

Soon they were enjoying their feast of crusty rolls and fresh apple juice. Sally had brought some of her mum's cakes for herself and Emma. They were delicious.

Emma gave Sheltie and Minnow some chunks of apple and carrot that

Mum had packed in a plastic bag for her.

After lunch, the girls climbed back into their saddles and set off for a walk across the moors.

There were dozens of sheep standing in groups. And lots of lambs. Some of them were still a bit wobbly on their legs.

'That one looks really soft and fluffy,' said Emma. 'Just like a little cloud.'

'Look at that lamb over there sniffing that flower,' said Sally. 'I wonder if the farmer names the lambs? I'd call that one Blossom!'

Sheltie blew a raspberry, as if to say, what a silly name!

The girls laughed.

Suddenly Sheltie stopped walking.

His ears pricked up and his head tilted slightly as if he were listening to something.

'What is it, Sheltie?' asked Emma.

Sheltie gave a loud whinny and looked all around. Minnow's ears pricked up too. Then the girls heard it. It was a tiny bleating noise.

'Where is it coming from?' asked Sally.

The noise got a little louder. It didn't sound like a normal happy bleat. It didn't sound very nice at all.

'*Baaaaaaaaaa! Baaaaa!*'

'It sounds like a sheep in pain,' said Emma.

Sheltie listened carefully. Then he turned and walked slowly towards some bushes near by.

There was a sheep half hidden by
the bushes. She was lying on her side
and she looked very unhappy. The
sheep raised her head, looked up at
Sheltie and bleated pitifully.

Chapter Three

Emma quickly slid out of the saddle and handed Sheltie's reins to Sally. Then she knelt down beside the sheep.

'Poor thing,' said Emma. 'I wonder what's wrong with her?'

'Her tummy is moving,' said Sally.

They watched as the sheep's tummy jumped. Then the sheep gave another bleat.

'She must be having a lamb,' said
Emma. 'It looks as if something is
wrong. I think she might be in
trouble.'

'What shall we do?' said Sally.

The sheep gave another loud bleat.

'We must get help,' said Emma.

'Yes,' agreed Sally. 'And fast!'

'But we can't leave her all alone,'
said Emma. 'If Sheltie and I ride for
help, do you think you could stay with
her until we come back, Sally?'

'OK,' Sally replied. 'But there's not
much I can do.'

'We'll be as quick as we can,' said
Emma. 'Just keep talking to her!'

Emma climbed into the saddle and
prodded Sheltie gently with her heels
to get him moving. Soon they were

galloping as fast as they could. Emma held on tightly as Sheltie's little hoofs pounded across the moor.

There were some fields at the edge of the moor and Sheltie headed for those. They followed a wide track, which Emma knew led down to Burdock Farm.

The farmhouse was a low stone building in the centre of a large cobbled yard. There was an enormous barn to one side.

Sheltie and Emma rode into the yard and were soon surrounded by hens and ducks, all clucking and fluttering excitedly at the new arrivals.

Sheltie stood very still while Emma dismounted. Just then a man came out of the back door of the farmhouse.

'Hello there,' he said. 'I wondered what all the commotion was about.'

'I'm Emma and this is Sheltie. We were riding on the moor with my friend,' said Emma, 'and we found a sheep in trouble. Can you help?'

'Yes, show me the way,' said the farmer. Then he called, 'Joe, come quickly!'

Joe came running out of the house. 'Oh, hello, Emma. What are you doing here?'

'Emma's found a poorly sheep on the moor,' said Joe's father. 'And we're going to have a look. I'll be back soon.'

Emma pulled herself back into Sheltie's saddle and waited while the farmer climbed on to his tractor.

Then Emma and Sheltie led Mr

Tomlinson back to where they'd left
Sally and Minnow with the sheep.

'Oh, Emma, at last! I'm so glad
you're back,' said Sally. 'The poor
thing is making terrible noises and I
don't know what to do.'

Sheltie nuzzled Sally's cheek and
whickered gently.

'It's all right,' said the farmer. 'I'm
here now.'

He knelt down beside the sheep and
looked her over.

'It's Nellie,' he said. 'Looks like she's having trouble birthing her lamb.'

'Nellie!' said Emma. 'Oh no!'

'Mr Thorne, the vet, said he was going over to Whitestone Farm when I saw him earlier,' said Mr Tomlinson. 'But I need his help now. Do either of you girls know the way to Whitestone Farm?'

'I've been there once with Dad,' said Emma. 'I'm sure that Sheltie and I can find it.'

'Good girl,' said the farmer. 'Can you bring Mr Thorne back here?'

Emma urged Sheltie into a gallop. They passed the track that led back to Burdock Farm and followed a path that eventually led down to the main road.

Emma pulled the reins to stop Sheltie at the edge of the road, checking for traffic. They turned left and trotted along the grass verge next to the road. Soon they came to a fork in the road, with three roads leading off.

'I can't remember which way it is, Sheltie,' said Emma.

Sheltie tossed his head and looked all round. Emma didn't know what to do next.

'Which way should we go?'

Suddenly they heard the sound of an engine coming towards them. Emma gripped Sheltie's reins tightly in one hand and waved her other arm frantically.

Sheltie gave a loud whinny and stamped his hoofs.

A Land Rover stopped, the door opened and a man jumped down.

Sheltie seemed to recognize Mr Thorne at once and trotted towards him. He came to a sudden stop right in front of the vet and nearly knocked him off balance.

'Mr Thorne!' gasped Emma. She had never been so pleased to see anyone in her life.

'Hello, Emma,' said the vet. 'What's up?' he asked when he saw her worried face.

'There's a sheep about to have a lamb but she's in trouble. We fetched Mr Tomlinson, but he needs your help,' said Emma. 'Please come quickly.'

'Show me the way,' said Mr Thorne,

climbing back into the Land Rover. 'I'll follow you.'

Emma pulled gently on Sheltie's reins to turn him and then they trotted back along the way they had come, with Mr Thorne following.

When they arrived, the vet jumped out of the Land Rover and grabbed his

bag. He knelt beside Mr Tomlinson
and examined Nellie carefully.

'Her lamb is stuck,' said the vet. 'But
I can help it. Don't worry.'

Sheltie swished his tail. Mr Thorne
had helped him many times.

'Why don't you girls take the ponies
for a little walk,' suggested Mr
Tomlinson. 'I'm sure everything will
be all right.'

The two girls walked Sheltie and
Minnow away from Nellie's bleats.
They were very worried about the ewe
and her lamb and didn't want to go
far while they waited for news.

Suddenly there was a shout from Mr
Tomlinson.

'Come and see the baby lamb, girls!'
Emma and Sally turned the ponies

and ran back with them as fast as they
could.

The newborn lamb was so adorable.
Nellie was busy licking it. Sheltie
lowered his head and nuzzled the
baby lamb. It gave a little bleat and
licked his nose.

'Is it all right?' asked Emma anxiously.

'It's fine now,' said Mr Thorne. 'And so is Nellie.'

'I think we should name the lamb "Baby Sheltie",' said Mr Tomlinson. 'After all, Emma tells me it was Sheltie who found Nellie in the bushes.'

Sheltie tossed his head and gave a loud whinny as if to say, 'Now that *is* a good name!'

Chapter Four

One morning, a week later, Emma
woke up early. She dressed for school
and rushed downstairs. She pulled on
her boots by the kitchen door and
hurried outside to feed Sheltie. There
was a very fine drizzle of rain this
morning and the ground was a little
muddy.

Emma opened the paddock gate and
closed it after her. She made her way

over to Sheltie's field shelter to feed
him his pony mix.

Sheltie knew it was time for
breakfast and galloped around the
paddock excitedly.

Suddenly something woolly came
tearing down the lane. Big drops of
mud splattered behind it as it dashed
towards the paddock. It was followed
by something smaller, but equally fast.

It was a fluffy sheep and a small
lamb!

Sheltie gave a loud whinny of
greeting.

'It's Nellie and Baby Sheltie,' cried
Emma.

'Come back, Nellie!' cried Joe, racing
along the lane behind them.

The sheep and lamb ducked under

the paddock fence, dashed across the field and ran into the shelter. Sheltie gave a loud blow and rushed in after them.

A few moments later he came prancing out followed by Nellie and her lamb. Then Sheltie trotted around the paddock with mother and baby trotting behind him. They made Emma and Joe laugh because they looked so funny. It was as if they were playing

follow the leader, with Sheltie in charge.

'I'm glad you all came to visit,' said Emma.

'Mr Crock saw Nellie heading this way and phoned us again,' said Joe. 'I brought this with me,' he added. Joe handed Emma a large parcel wrapped in brown paper. 'It's from my mum and dad, to say thank you for your help with Nellie's lamb.'

Emma pulled off the sticky tape at each end and opened the brown paper parcel carefully. Inside was something large and soft. Emma pulled it out and shook it open.

'It's a new wool blanket for Sheltie,' said Joe.

'Oh, thank you,' said Emma. 'Isn't it

lovely, Sheltie?' She held his blanket
up for him to see. A picture of a
Shetland pony's head was woven into
one corner.

Sheltie trotted over to have a look.
He swished his tail from side to side.
The lamb followed him. It gave a little
bleat and tried to nibble the edge of
the blanket.

'I think it's time to take Nellie and
Baby Sheltie home,' said Joe.

He knelt down and held out his
hand. Baby Sheltie bounded towards
him and sucked his outstretched
thumb. Then Nellie ambled over for
some fussing and Joe slipped the collar
over her head. Joe knew a lot about
sheep and lambs.

'Doesn't Baby Sheltie have a collar

to wear like Nellie?' asked Emma.

'There's no need,' said Joe. 'He'll always follow his mother. Come on, Sheltie, let's go.'

Sheltie's ears pricked up when he heard his name and he raced over to the fence. He tossed his head and gave a loud snort.

Joe and Emma laughed.

'Not *you*, Sheltie,' said Emma. 'Joe was calling Baby Sheltie, the lamb!'

Little Lamb
Lost

Chapter One

It was a warm spring Saturday. It had been raining all day and every day for the past week. This was the first dry, sunny day for ages, and Emma was in the paddock grooming Sheltie.

She carefully untangled a mess of knots in his shaggy mane and long tail. Emma wanted Sheltie to look his very best today because Joe Tomlinson had invited them over to his house,

Burdock Farm, for tea.

'Sheltie looks very handsome today,' said Mum. 'And I think it's time you got yourself ready now, Emma.'

'OK,' said Emma. 'I won't be long, Sheltie.' Emma hurried into the cottage to change.

Sheltie gave an impatient blow. He was tired of being cooped up in his paddock. It had been raining so much lately that he hadn't been for any long rides anywhere.

A baby blackbird fluttered out of its nest in the cherry tree and swooped clumsily up on to the paddock fence.

It seemed that the baby blackbirds were learning to fly. They weren't very good at it yet. The mother bird flew out of the nest, followed by the second

baby bird, who fluttered past Sheltie's head. Then he followed his mother and brother, fluttering across the paddock.

Emma appeared at the kitchen door. She pulled on her riding boots and straightened her hat. Then she opened the gate and hurried into the paddock with Sheltie's tack.

'I think we're all ready to go now, Sheltie,' said Emma when she had finished.

Sheltie blew a raspberry. He was eager to be off for his ride.

Emma climbed into the saddle and squeezed her heels to send Sheltie trotting out of the paddock.

Sheltie gave an excited whinny as they trotted down the lane.

Emma and Sheltie followed the long bridle path which led through Bramble Woods. The path went all the way up to where the downs met the moor.

Emma urged Sheltie into a gallop when they left the woods and let him have a good run across the open grassland.

They rode along the edge of the

downs and up a steep slope. Sheltie
came to a sudden stop at the top.

'Why did you stop, Sheltie?' asked
Emma.

Sheltie snorted and remained still.

Emma looked down and saw the
steep bank leading down to the river.
The heavy rain they'd had over the
last few days had made the ground

very slippery. The river was swollen
and almost flooding the bank. Some of
the plants that grew along the edge
were being washed away by the force
of the water.

'Oh, Sheltie,' said Emma. 'It's lucky
you stopped when you did.'

Sheltie blew a troubled snort and
took a few steps back, away from the
edge. As he moved his feet, a huge
blob of mud fell away from the edge
and splattered down the bank. Emma
gripped Sheltie's reins tightly. It was
frightening to see how slippery the
ground was.

'I think we'd better ride away from
here,' said Emma.

She drew in Sheltie's reins and
turned him carefully. Emma was

terrified that Sheltie might slip and fall. The little pony seemed eager to get away from the edge too. He pulled forward, trying to break into a trot. Emma held him back with all her strength.

'No, Sheltie, we must be careful.'

Sheltie jangled his bit and stopped pulling so hard on the reins.

They walked slowly back down the way they had come and then trotted to the track that led from the moor to Joe Tomlinson's farm.

The farmhouse was a low stone building surrounded by a cobbled yard. They rode up to the farmhouse and Emma climbed out of the saddle. She still felt a little shaky from the danger on the hill as she tethered

Sheltie loosely to the low wooden fence that ran around the yard.

'Hello, Emma,' called Mrs Tomlinson, poking her head out of the back door of the farmhouse and giving Emma a wave. 'Joe is in the barn.'

Emma waved back and walked over to the barn. She shoved the huge wooden doors open enough to peek inside.

'Joe!' she called.

'Here.' Joe appeared from the darkness, pushing back his curly hair with one hand. 'Hello, Emma, I was just tidying some empty sacks for my dad. Come inside and help me if you like.'

Joe led Emma into the barn. It was quite dark inside. There were lots of cobwebs and Emma noticed little specks of dust floating in the air where the light shone in long shafts through the cracks of the wooden doors.

Joe picked up an armful of empty sacks and began folding them in half. Emma noticed a loud noise coming from a big pile of hay in the corner of the barn.

'What's that?' asked Emma.

'That's Henrietta, our pig,' said Joe with a cheeky grin. Henrietta was an old pot-bellied pig who was lying on the hay. She was very big and very fat. She was fast asleep and snoring loudly. Emma laughed as she picked up some sacks and helped Joe to fold them in a neat pile.

'Dad told me to let Sheltie have the

run of our paddock while you're here,' said Joe when they'd finished tidying the sacks. 'We don't have any horses, so it's empty at the moment.'

'Sheltie will love that,' said Emma. 'I left him tied to the yard fence.'

'Let's take him into the paddock then,' said Joe.

'It's a shame you don't have horses or ponies,' said Emma. 'If you did, you could come for long rides with Sheltie and me.'

'I know. You're very lucky to have Sheltie,' said Joe. 'My dad has promised to buy me a pony for my birthday the next time he goes to the livestock auctions. Still, at least we've got a lamb called Baby Sheltie, named after a very special pony!'

They walked over and untied
Sheltie's reins from the fence. Joe
showed Emma and Sheltie a lovely big
paddock at the back of the barn. It was
nearly three times as big as Sheltie's
paddock at home. Sheltie dashed off in

a mad gallop around it as soon as he was inside.

Then he gave a loud whinny and charged back towards Joe and Emma. He galloped around them, then dashed back to the other end.

'I think Sheltie likes your paddock,' laughed Emma.

Chapter Two

They closed the paddock gate and walked back towards the farmyard. Sheltie followed them along the length of the paddock fence. Then he rested his fuzzy chin on the top bar to watch the farmyard animals.

The farmyard was full of ducks and hens waddling and fluttering about.

'Would you like to feed them?' asked Joe.

'Can I?' said Emma.

'Of course,' said Joe. He disappeared into the barn and came back a few moments later with a bucketful of grain and a large carrot poking out of his pocket. He picked up a handful of grain and threw it on to the cobbles. 'Do it like this.'

Emma reached into the bucket and took a handful of grain. She copied Joe and threw it to the ducks over near the paddock fence.

The ducks quacked and squabbled for the grain. Sheltie shuffled back out of their way with a whimpering snort.

'I nearly forgot,' said Joe. 'I brought you a carrot, Sheltie.' He palmed it to the little Shetland pony. Sheltie crunched it noisily.

'Joe, Emma,' called Joe's mum from the kitchen door. 'Time for tea!'

They hurried inside to wash their hands. Joe's mum gave them thick-crust beef pie, mashed potatoes with loads of gravy, baby carrots, and a big red jelly for pudding. It was delicious.

After tea, Mr Tomlinson took them for a ride around the farm on his tractor. They saw two fields full of corn shoots and a meadow with some cows who were grazing happily. They rode right up to the moor to see the Tomlinsons' sheep and then rode back again.

Emma had a lovely time and thanked Mrs Tomlinson for inviting her. Then it was time to start the ride home. She fetched Sheltie from the paddock and, holding his reins in one hand, climbed into the saddle.

Joe waved as Emma and Sheltie trotted off.

A fine mist had started to drift over the ground. It made the moor look a bit creepy.

'Come on, Sheltie,' said Emma. 'Let's hurry.'

She nudged Sheltie gently with her heels and urged him into a gallop across the moor.

But the mist grew thicker and thicker as they rode, and soon Emma couldn't see very far ahead. They were surrounded by white fog.

Sheltie slowed to a walk. He *seemed* to know where he was going, and Emma trusted that Sheltie would be

able to find his way home, even
though he couldn't see clearly.
Normally, Sheltie could lead the way
by recognizing familiar scents. But
there was nothing at all familiar on
this side of the moor. The mist had
come down so suddenly, and it was
impossible to see anything.

'I'm not sure where we are, Sheltie,'
said Emma. 'I think we might be lost.'

Sheltie shook his mane and whickered softly.

Emma pulled on the reins to stop him. It was frightening, not being able to see where they were going.

'I think we should wait here until the mist clears a bit,' said Emma.

Sheltie stood very still while Emma slipped down from the saddle. She led him over to some rocks that she could see near by and sat down. Emma held the reins loosely in one hand. Sheltie bent his head and nibbled on the long grass while he waited.

Suddenly, Sheltie's ears pricked up. He tossed his head and looked this way and that. He nudged Emma with his nose.

'What is it, Sheltie?' she asked.

Sheltie's ears twitched and he gave a loud blow.

Emma listened carefully and suddenly could hear a soft bleating noise. It sounded quite far away.

'It sounds like a lamb,' said Emma. 'Do you think it's lost like us?'

Sheltie pulled on the reins in Emma's hand and sniffed the air.

'Let's try to find it,' said Emma. 'We might as well all be lost together.'

Chapter Three

Emma and Sheltie walked in the direction that the bleating seemed to be coming from. Emma looked at the ground as they walked, to make sure the footing was safe for Sheltie.

The bleating got louder and Sheltie pulled forward, almost yanking the reins out of Emma's hand. She gripped them tightly and let Sheltie lead her up a steep slope.

Sheltie whinnied as he scrambled up to the top.

Emma could hardly see a thing now, the mist was so thick. And she was starting to feel very cold. Apart from the lamb bleating, the moor was silent.

The bleating was very close now. It sounded as if it was coming from just below them. Emma looked across over the top of Sheltie's saddle. She could just see the beginning of a drop on the other side of the bank and could hear water gushing below them.

'I know where we are, Sheltie!' she cried. 'This is the river bank.'

Sheltie pawed at the ground. And the lost lamb made a loud bleating noise just below them.

'The lamb must have slipped down there,' said Emma.

She knelt on the grass and looked over the edge. Just below her, Emma could see a muddy ridge with a little lamb curled up in a hollow. It was bleating pitifully.

'*Baaaaa!*'

'It's all right,' said Emma. 'We'll help you.'

Emma stretched out her arms, but she couldn't quite reach the lamb. As she leaned towards it, she dislodged a large rock which slithered down the muddy bank and plopped into the river below.

Emma pulled back from the edge. Maybe it would be safer to coax the lamb towards her. The lamb was very

small and couldn't weigh much.
Emma was sure the ground would be
firm enough for it to climb up.

'It's lucky you landed there and
didn't go sliding down to the river,
little lamb,' she told it. 'Come here.

Come on.' Emma held out her hand and made soft, kissing noises.

The lamb struggled up on to its feet and looked up at her.

'*Baaaaa!*' It was very frightened. Emma could see its legs trembling.

'Come on,' urged Emma gently. 'Come to me.'

The lamb just stood there looking up at her.

'Baaaaa,' Emma made a bleating noise to try to get the lamb to come towards her, but it was no good. The lamb was just too frightened.

'What shall we do, Sheltie?' said Emma.

Sheltie took a step forward. Then another one. His front legs were now right on the edge of the bank. It was very slippery but the sturdy little pony managed to keep his footing.

'Be careful, Sheltie!' cried Emma.

Sheltie snorted. He took another careful step and then bent his head, pulling the reins from Emma's hand. Sheltie was determined to help. He could just reach the little lamb from there. He stretched his neck forward and nudged the lamb along with his nose. The lamb took a step up towards Emma, but still she couldn't reach it. Sheltie nudged the lamb again. This time it took two steps towards Emma.

Now the lamb was close enough for Emma to reach it. She grabbed its little front legs and pulled it gently into her arms. The baby lamb curled against her, shaking with fright.

'You're safe now,' whispered Emma, hugging it close.

Sheltie stepped back slowly to where the ground was less slippery. Emma tucked the little lamb inside her jacket and led Sheltie down to the bottom of the slope.

It was getting very chilly and the

mist was still thick. The mist clung to
Emma's hair and clothes. She was
feeling very worried. The mist wasn't
clearing at all. She found some shelter
by feeling around until she touched an
overhanging rock. She sat down under
it, hoping that the mist would soon
clear.

Sheltie stood close to Emma. His
thick coat felt nice and warm. He
nuzzled her neck and gave her a little
lick.

'Are you worried too, Sheltie?' she
asked as he pressed his side against
her.

It seemed like hours passed as they
huddled together. Emma didn't feel
well. Her hands were so cold, they felt

numb, even though she'd stuffed them in her pockets to try to keep them warm. The little lamb went to sleep with its head tucked under Emma's arm.

Suddenly Sheltie's ears pricked up and he gave a very loud neigh.

Emma could hear something in the distance. It was very faint but it sounded like someone calling her name. Then she heard it again, louder this time. And she saw the faint glow of a light shining through the mist.

'Emma! Sheltie!'

'Here, we're over here!' cried Emma.

Sheltie gave an enormous series of loud whinnies.

'Thank goodness I've found you!' said Mr Tomlinson, as he emerged

from the swirling mist to stand right in
front of them. He carried an oil lamp
with him. 'We've all been so worried
about you. The mist came down over
the farm shortly after you left. Then
your dad telephoned to say you hadn't
arrived home yet and it was getting
late.'

'We got lost,' said Emma. 'We found
this baby lamb too. It had slipped

down on to the river bank.'

'Your dad is searching Bramble
Woods for you. I'd better let everyone
know you're safe,' said Mr Tomlinson.

Mr Tomlinson had a mobile phone
with him. He phoned home and told
his wife that he had found them.

'Mrs Tomlinson is going to phone
your mum and dad to tell them you're
safe. The mist is too thick for us to
take you home tonight. You and
Sheltie can stay at the farm and make
your way home tomorrow, after the
mist has cleared,' said Mr Tomlinson.

Emma handed the little lamb to Mr
Tomlinson and climbed up into
Sheltie's saddle. Mr Tomlinson held on
to the reins with one hand and tucked
the lamb under his other arm. He led

them all across the moors and back to the farm.

'It's lucky you know your way across the moor so well, Mr Tomlinson,' said Emma.

'I used this compass to help me find my way around tonight,' said Mr Tomlinson. He held up the shiny compass for Emma to see.

Mrs Tomlinson ushered Emma into the warm kitchen as soon as they arrived back at the farm.

'But I have to take care of Sheltie,' said Emma.

'It's all right,' said Mr Tomlinson. 'I'll take Sheltie to the paddock and settle him in. You stay and get warm. Here, you can take the lamb inside too. We'll see about returning it to its mother tomorrow.'

Chapter Four

The next morning, Emma woke up in the Tomlinsons' spare room. She sat up slowly and rubbed her sleepy eyes, wondering where she was. Then she remembered what had happened. She got up and looked out of the window and saw that the cloudless sky was as blue as cornflowers and the sun was shining brightly. There was no sign of the mist at all.

She dressed quickly and hurried downstairs.

'It's all right,' said Joe. 'Sheltie is already having his breakfast. Dad and I fed him about five minutes ago.'

'I just want to say good morning to him, then I'll be right back,' said Emma.

'Hurry up,' said Mrs Tomlinson. 'Breakfast's nearly ready.'

Emma dashed outside and over to the paddock. Sheltie was busy munching a pony mix from a trough in the corner.

'Morning, Sheltie,' she called.

Sheltie lifted his head and gave a loud belch.

'You *are* funny, Sheltie,' said Emma. 'Anyone would think you haven't eaten for a week. Slow down or you'll get a tummy ache.'

Sheltie stuck his head back in the trough and gobbled up the rest of his breakfast.

Mrs Tomlinson had cooked bacon and eggs. A wonderful smell filled the kitchen and Emma's tummy gave a loud growl as she sat down at the large wooden table, making everyone laugh.

'I'm starving,' said Emma.

'Well, tuck in,' said Mrs Tomlinson. She put a plate in front of Emma, filled with bacon, eggs and sausages.

'There's heaps of toast,' said Joe.

Emma wolfed down her breakfast and ate three slices of toast spread with thick home-made marmalade.

After breakfast, Emma and Joe helped to wash and dry the dishes. Then Emma went out to the paddock to get Sheltie ready for the ride home.

She was just climbing into the saddle when Joe and Mr Tomlinson joined her. Joe was carrying the little lamb.

'We thought we'd walk across the moor with you,' said Mr Tomlinson. 'To see you safely back as far as Bramble Woods.'

'And we're taking the lamb back to his mother on the way,' said Joe.

'I bet the ewe has been very worried about her lamb,' said Emma.

They set off at a gentle pace along the track leading to the moor.

Every time they saw a group of
sheep, Joe would put the little lamb
down and push him forward to find
his mother. But none of the sheep
seemed at all interested in him. Each
time he ran back and huddled close to
Sheltie's legs.

'Maybe he thinks Sheltie is his
mother,' said Emma.

'I'm sure he'll know his mother when he sees her,' said Joe.

Suddenly there was a loud bleating and a big fluffy sheep came charging towards them at a hundred miles an hour.

'I know who *that* is!' cried Emma. 'That's Lightning Nellie, the runaway sheep!'

Nellie bounded towards them. Sheltie gave a loud blow of greeting and danced back, out of Nellie's way.

'I wonder where her lamb is,' said Joe.

Sheltie whickered softly and nudged the little lamb with his nose.

'Sheltie thinks the lost lamb is Nellie's,' said Emma.

Joe put the lamb down. This time it

didn't run back to Sheltie. It ran
straight towards Nellie. It was bleating
like mad. The lost little lamb was
Nellie's baby!

'It was Baby Sheltie all the time!'
cried Emma. 'And we never knew.'

'No wonder he got lost,' said Joe.
'He must have lost Nellie in the fog
and wandered off,' said Joe. 'I hope

he's not going to grow up to be a wandering sheep like his mum!'

Sheltie blew a raspberry, and made everyone laugh.

Joe and his dad headed back to the farm once they had reached the edge of Bramble Woods. They waved goodbye to Sheltie and Emma as they trotted off through the woods and made their way home.

Little Joshua came running down the garden as Emma led Sheltie back into his own paddock.

Sheltie seemed pleased to be home.

'Sheltie,' called Joshua.

Sheltie swished his tail and gave Joshua a friendly neigh.

'Welcome home,' said Dad. 'I hear

you had quite an adventure on the moor.'

'We did,' said Emma. 'And we had a great time at the Tomlinsons'. But it's nice to be home.'

Emma removed Sheltie's bridle. She hung his saddle over the top bar of the fence and watched as he galloped around the paddock, shaking out his mane.

'It's good to have you both back,' said Dad. 'We missed you. It was so quiet.'

Just then the baby blackbirds fluttered into the paddock, squabbling noisily over a fat worm.

'It certainly isn't quiet now,' said Emma. 'I think Sheltie is glad to be home, anyway, aren't you, Sheltie?'

Sheltie gave a very noisy blow, and
rolled over and over in the grass.